QUIZ NO:-

Little
HORRORS

Shiver with fear...

Owwl!

...shake with laughter!

Visit Shoo Rayner's website!
www.shoo-rayner.co.uk

ORCHARD BOOKS
96 Leonard Street, London EC2A 4XD
Orchard Books Australia
32/45-51 Huntley Street, Alexandria, NSW 2015
First published in Great Britain in 2003
First paperback edition 2004
Copyright © Shoo Rayner 2003
The right of Shoo Rayner to be identified as the author
and illustrator of this work has been asserted by him in
accordance with the Copyright, Designs, and Patents Act, 1988.
A CIP catalogue record for this book is available
from the British Library.
ISBN 1 84362 008 1 (hardback)
ISBN 1 84362 012 X (paperback)
1 3 5 7 9 10 8 6 4 2 (hardback)
1 3 5 7 9 10 8 6 4 2 (paperback)
Printed in Great Britain

Little HORRORS

The Shadow Man

Shoo Rayner

ORCHARD BOOKS

Nothing could save me. Aliens were attacking on all sides!

"Sam!" screamed my sister, Kim. "Slam on your retro thrusters!"

I pressed the triangle and wrenched back the joystick.

It worked…the aliens flew right underneath me and smashed into an asteroid.

"Phew! Thanks, Sis," I gasped. "I really thought I was finished that time."

The door flew open and Mum barged in.

"Look at all this mess! I want this place cleaned up before Dad gets home."

Dad had been away all week. We were looking forward to seeing him.

Kim pressed quit. The room went dark, except for two green blinking eyes that stared out of the screen. A deep, creepy voice filled the room.

It was an advert for another
game called Shadow Man. It looked
so scary.

As we began to tidy up, Mum flung the curtains open. Sunshine poured into the room.

"Beware of the shadows, indeed!"
she said sarcastically. "You spend
half your lives playing those games
in the shadows. If you're not careful,
your brains will rot!"

Mum said we needed to get out in the sunshine and get some fresh air. She made us go to the shops for her.

I had the strangest feeling in the supermarket - it was like someone was watching us. But when I looked behind, there was no one there.

I nudged Kim. "Do you feel like we're being watched?"

Kim just laughed. "Mum's right, those video games are rotting your brain!"

Maybe it was true. I even thought the beeps of the checkout sounded like an alien detector!

On our way out, I thought I saw a shadow move behind the closed curtains of the passport photo-booth.

I sneaked towards it…

…ready to jerk the curtain back.

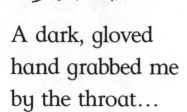

A dark, gloved hand grabbed me by the throat…

…and dragged me inside!

I glimpsed my terrified reflection
in the lens of the camera.

Before the flash lights exploded, I saw the mad, staring eyes of my attacker.

His laugh made my legs turn to jelly.

Blinded, I struggled to get free.

As my sight came back, a mad, grinning face swayed in front of my bleary eyes.

"Jamie!" I growled at my school friend. "I might have known it was you." Jamie loves playing tricks.

"Always beware of the shadows!" he said mysteriously.

If we weren't in the supermarket, I'd have made Jamie beware of the shadows for good!

He was wearing a Shadow Man T-shirt. He told us he'd already got the Shadow Man game.

"Why don't you come and play it this afternoon?" he suggested. He dropped his voice to a whisper. "It's really scary!"

A weird grinding noise made us jump out of our skins.

We-e-e-erk!

It was the photos. I looked terrified, but Jamie was just a blurred shadow, trying to strangle me.

We took the shopping to Mum. She let us go to Jamie's as long as we were back before Dad came home. We didn't tell her why we were going!

Shadow Man was brilliant. You never really saw him as you moved around the screen, only in your imagination…that's much more scary!

The Shadow
Man followed
you everywhere.
You could hear
him breathe.

You could hear
his skittering
footsteps.

His green
glowing eyes
blinked
slowly in
the darkness.

We looked for clues to help us escape the Shadow Man. We heard him creep behind us, waiting to pounce and grab us in his strangling, suffocating grip.

Then Kim found an escape route. She had to go carefully. If she trod on the wrong stepping stone, she'd set off the alarms. Then the Shadow Man would get her.

Jamie and I held our breath.

As Kim chose the next stepping stone, a loud noise filled the room.

"Argh!" Kim threw the controller
in the air.

Jamie fell about laughing. "It's the
phone, stupid!"

Bleeh!
Bleeh!

It was Dad, calling to say that he was home and Mum was hopping mad with us!

"Arrrgh! We're late for tea. We'll have to run all the way." I looked at Kim. "W-w-we'll have to go the short cut...d-d-d-down Back Lane!"

"Back Lane, eh?" whispered Jamie. "Don't forget to beware of the shadows!"

I wish he hadn't said that. It was dark in Back Lane.

Kim clutched my hand…

…We tiptoed down the pavement.

It was like the Shadow World.

Shadows moved in the hedges.

Shadows moved behind gates.

Shadows moved behind cars.

Someone breathed heavily. Was it me or Kim…or someone else?!

Two green eyes blinked out at me from the shadows.

As Kim hissed, "Quiet! Don't make a noise!" I tripped, fell and crashed into a dustbin. Rubbish flew everywhere. The dustbin clanged and clattered down the street.

I lay amongst the spilled rubbish.
Something wailed in the tree
above me.

It landed on my back.

I just caught sight of its wild, green eyes before it had me in a strangling, suffocating grip. I screamed, but no sound came out!

Then, in an instant, it was gone.
Vanished into the dark, silent,
looming shadows.

We didn't wait a moment longer.
We ran and ran, lungs bursting, legs
aching.

Dad was emptying the boot of the car as we came tearing around the corner.

"Hey, you were quick" he said. "W-w-w-we ran all the way," we panted. "We wanted to see you!"

"Oh that's nice," he smiled. "Look, I've brought you a present. I think it's the kind of thing you like."

Kim and I opened the bag.
Instantly, we recognised the familiar
design on the box…

> Look out for these brilliant books from Orchard!

Little Horrors by Shoo Rayner

❏ The Swamp Man	1 84121 646 1	£3.99
❏ The Pumpkin Man	1 84121 644 5	£3.99
❏ The Spider Man	1 84121 648 8	£3.99
❏ The Sand Man	1 84121 650 X	£3.99
❏ The Snow Man	1 84362 009 X	£3.99
❏ The Bone Man	1 84362 010 3	£3.99
❏ The Bogey Man	1 84362 011 1	£3.99
❏ The Shadow Man	1 84362 012 X	£3.99

Finger Clicking Reads by Shoo Rayner

❏ Rock-a-doodle-do!	1 84121 465 5	£3.99
❏ Treacle, Treacle, Little Tart	1 84121 469 8	£3.99

The One and Only by Laurence Anholt and Tony Ross

❏ Micky the Muckiest Boy	1 86039 983 5	£3.99
❏ Ruby the Rudest Girl	1 86039 623 2	£3.99
❏ Harold the Hairiest Man	1 86039 624 0	£3.99

And many more!